Look for these

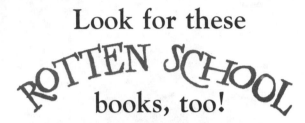

ROTTEN SCHOOL
books, too!

The Big
Blueberry
Barf-Off!

The Great
Smelling Bee

The Good,
the Bad and
the Very Slimy

ROTTEN SCHOOL

GROWTH LEARNING PIZZA!

LOSE, TEAM, LOSE!

R.L. STINE

Illustrations by Trip Park

HarperCollins*Publishers*
A Parachute Press Book

For Lawson
–TP

Library of Congress Cataloging-in-Publication Data
Stine, R. L.
Lose, team, lose! / R.L. Stine ; illustrations by Trip Park.— 1st ed.
    p. cm. — (Rotten School ; 4)
"A Parachute Press Book."
Summary: The biggest, toughest girl in school joins the football team and foils a sly
fourth grader's attempts to win the affections of the snobbiest girl in the class.
    ISBN-10: 0-06-078808-9 (trade bdg.)—ISBN-10: 0-06-078809-7 (lib. bdg.)
    ISBN-13: 978-0-06-078808-7 (trade bdg.)—ISBN-13: 978-0-06-078809-4 (lib. bdg.)
    1. Football—Fiction. 2. Boarding schools—Fiction. 3. Schools—Fiction.] I. Park, Trip,
ill. II. Title. III. Series.
PZ7.S86037Los 2006   2005018354
[Fic]—dc22   CIP
                                                                                    AC

Cover and interior design by mjcdesign
3 4 5 6 7 8 9 10
❖
First Edition

—·: CONTENTS :·—

Morning Announcements 1

1. Rotten Apples Roll! 4

2. Throw Up #6 9

3. Snack Time for the Quarterback 13

4. Sherman Laughs and Laughs 18

5. A New Cheer for April-May 24

6. Honey Bucket Has an Idea 29

7. Advice from Coach Bunz 36

8. A Great Pep Talk 40

9. The Secret Weapon 45

10. Attack of the Ecch 50

11. Big News from April-May 58

12. What Rhymes with Ecch? 62

13. Sherman's Evil Plot 68

14. Am I Doomed or Am I Doomed? 74

15. How to Beat Maniacs 78

16. Sherman Feels Sorry 83

17. Huge Boys 86

18. The New All-Stars 89

19. The Ecch Problem 94

20. Doomed 98

21. The Knitting Needles Fly 103

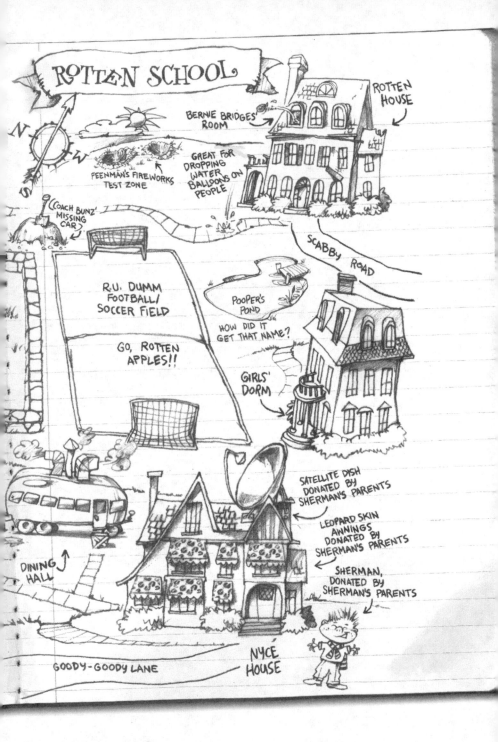

MORNING ANNOUNCEMENTS

Good morning, Rotten Students. This is Headmaster Upchuck. Let's make this day a Rotten Day for everyone!

Here are your Morning Announcements. Try to listen, if you can....

Nyce House fourth grader Wes Updood had his appendix removed last Saturday. He will be showing off his icky red scars during dinner tonight in the Dining Hall.

A reminder from our wonderful Dining Hall cook, Chef Baloney: "Spinach is a vegetable—not a throwing thing."

Nurse Hanley has important advice for all fifth graders: "If you keep picking at it, it won't heal."

Fifth grader Eric Spindlebag has won another essay contest. The topic of the contest was: WHAT OUR PLANET NEEDS TO SURVIVE. And Eric's essay won first prize in the nation. It was titled, "Please Go Away and Leave Me Alone."

Mrs. Twinkler, our Drama Coach, announces the school play will be a stage version of *Finding Nemo*. Students who would like to be in the play are urged to try out. Mrs. Twinkler is looking for kids who have fish faces. And you must know how to swim.

Our Fighting Apples football team will be playing the Backstabbers from SpongeBob SquarePants All-Faith Academy this afternoon on the R.U. Dumm Football Field. Coach Manley Bunz asks: "Will someone please come watch the game?"

As you know, our team has a 1,500-game losing streak. So let's all get out there and show them what we think of them!

Chapter 1

ROTTEN APPLES ROLL!

I call this story, "The Attack of the Ecch."

I can't tell you why right now. I'm in the middle of football practice.

What position do I play? Hey—do you really have to ask?

The quarterback has to be brilliant, quick, and good-looking, right? So they had no choice. It had to be me—Bernie Bridges.

I'll never forget the moment that Coach Manley Bunz handed me the football and told me I'd be leader of the team. He slapped me on the back and gave me his wonderful words of wisdom.

"Try not to get hurt," he said.

Thrilling words from a great coach.

I went running onto the practice field with that advice echoing in my ears. Coach Bunz shouted after me: "Don't break anything. It's the nurse's day off!"

This man knows how to motivate a team!

It takes a BIG man to coach a tough team of fourth and fifth graders. And Coach Bunz is a BIG man. He ran a race in the Teachers' Olympics last spring. And his stomach finished ten seconds before he did!

That's BIG—right?

Sometimes he gets the whole team in a huddle and he gives us a *real* pep talk. "You boys represent the Rotten School!" he shouts. "So I want you to get out on that field and show everyone what *rotten* means!"

The coach doesn't just fire us up. He also teaches us. "Don't do that!" he shouts. "Oh, *please*—don't do that!"

And that's how we learn.

"Go, Rotten Apples! Rotten Apples ROLL!"

That's the Official Team Cheer. Actually, we're known as the Fighting Apples.

But that's a problem. I mean, it's not a real *tough* football name. If you play football, you want your team to be named after a fierce animal, a killer bird, or a wild creature. You don't really want your team to be named after a FRUIT.

Well, okay. Bernie Bridges is man enough to face the truth. The Fighting Apples is *not* the best team in the Boarding School League. We lose all our games, we bleed a lot, and it usually isn't even close.

But we've got one thing going for us.

We have a *great* quarterback.

I thought I could turn these losers into a winning team. But I was wrong.

We didn't start winning until THE ATTACK OF THE ECCH.

Chapter 2

THROW UP #6

My story starts one week ago. It was a bright afternoon. The sun reflected off the grass of R.U. Dumm Football Field.

I got my guys into the huddle. The score was close. We were only losing 37 to 3.

Hey, that's a close game for us. And look who we were playing: one of the meanest, ugliest teams in the whole state—the Hammerhead Sharks from Lindsay Lohan Day School.

I had all my Rotten House buddies on the team. My best friends, Feenman and Crench, were the wide receivers. So far, they'd dropped twenty perfect passes.

I turned to them in the huddle. "Listen to your quarterback," I said. "You gotta start catching the ball. I know how to solve this problem."

"How, Bernie?" Crench asked.

"Turn your helmets around," I said.

They had their helmets on backwards. I helped them spin the helmets around.

"Hey, I can see!" Feenman cried.

"Wow! The sun is out!" Crench said, blinking. "I thought this was a *night* game!"

"You're a football genius, Big B!" Feenman cried.

"Save it for when you carry me out on your shoulders after the game," I said.

So far, we've lost every game. But they still insist on carrying me out on their shoulders. See? *That's* team spirit!

"Listen up. Feenman, do you know which side of the ball to catch?" I asked.

He thought. "That's a tough one, Bernie. Which side?"

"You catch the *outside*!" I said.

They all stared at me. "Dudes—that's a joke," I said.

A good quarterback knows how to keep his guys loose.

I turned to my friend Beast. Beast is our big, blocking lineman. He is huge and wide and hairy all over. Even his *forehead* is covered with bristly hair!

We're pretty sure Beast is human. But he grunts a lot and eats raw meat, and sometimes he chases cars.

"Beast, you gotta block for me," I said.

"Unnh-unnnh," he replied.

"Keep them all away from me," I told him. "Give me lots of time. Here's the play, guys. It's Throw Up Number Six."

"Throw Up Number Six?" Crench squinted at me. "Huh? What's that?"

"Simple," I said. "I throw the ball up to Number Six. That's you, Feenman."

"I thought that play is called Vomit Number Three," Crench said.

I shook my head. "No. That play is when I get sick on the sidelines."

I gave Crench a slap on the helmet. "Listen up."

"But, Bernie, why don't we try Hurl Number Four?" he asked. "You hurl the ball to *me*!"

"We'll try Hurl Number Four later," I said. "Now we're doing Throw Up Number Six. I take three steps back, count to five, and throw a long touchdown pass to Feenman."

I grabbed Beast's shoulder pad. "Can you block those guys?"

"GRRRRRR," he replied. He pulled back his lips and bared his teeth. They were all pointy.

I clapped my hands. "Okay, Beast is ready!" I shouted. "Are you ready, Apples? Let's go get 'em...."

Chapter 3

SNACK TIME FOR THE QUARTERBACK

Clapping my hands, I led the Fighting Apples up to the line.

The Hammerhead Sharks were waiting for us. Their helmets and uniforms were silvery gray, like sharks. They lowered themselves in place and prepared to attack.

"Hey, guys—nice uniforms!" I called out to them. "We've got *trash cans* that color! Ha-ha!"

They didn't move a muscle.

I could hear some of them gnashing their teeth, like sharks.

I started to feel a little tense.

These Sharks were BIG, and they all looked *hungry*.

"Hey, guys, do me a favor," I said. "Don't tackle too hard. I'm a bleeder!"

That didn't get a chuckle, either.

"It's a running play," I told them. "Right up the middle."

See? When you're a quarterback, you've got to use *strategy*. You've got to be tricky.

I turned to the sidelines. Coach Bunz was leaning forward with his hands on his knees, waiting for the play. James Jimmy James, the Yearbook photographer, stood next to him with his camera raised.

"Hey, Jimbo!" I shouted. "Move over. Get my good side. This isn't my good side. Take it from over there!"

Uh-oh. Everyone was tense. Waiting. Time to start the play.

I suddenly had doubts. Throw Up #6? Maybe that was the wrong play. Maybe we should try Upchuck #4, where I chuck the ball up to the closest runner. No time to change it. Here goes. "HIKE!" I yelled. I took the ball. I backed up three steps. I raised my arm and started to count. . . . "One . . . two . . ."

I saw Feenman run downfield.

He was open. He turned, ready to catch the ball. Yes! Yes!

"Three...four..."

Then I saw the dog run onto the field. A big, black Lab with a meat bone in its jaws.

I heard a growl. And I saw Beast drop to all fours and take off. *Beast went chasing after the dog!*

"Beast! You have to block!" I screamed.

Beast was growling too loud to hear me.

About twenty or thirty Sharks piled on me at once.

"Ooof!" I felt my breath knocked out in a whoosh. I went down hard, *smothered* under the pile of Sharks.

"Throw it! Bernie—heave it!" I heard Feenman shout.

But how could I *throw* when it was snack time for me? I was eating the *ball*!

Chapter 4

SHERMAN LAUGHS AND LAUGHS

Flat on my back, I waited for the Hammerhead Sharks to climb off. Then I stood up and the next thing I saw was Coach Bunz holding a pair of tongs. He worked very carefully with the tongs to pull the football from my throat.

"Cough it up," he said. "It's the only ball we have."

He lifted the ball out. Then he used a towel to wipe off the slobber—and the game continued.

We lost 55 to 3. My teammates carried me off the field on their shoulders.

A short while later, I trudged across the Rotten School campus, head down. I was on my way to Rotten House, my dorm. Every bone in my body ached.

I've got to do something *to help the team,* I thought. *Or else there's* no way *we'll survive the football season!*

A shadow fell over me. I looked up to see Sherman Oaks—that spoiled rich kid who rules the dorm we all hate: Nyce House. Sherman Oaks—my archenemy.

Sherman's blond hair was slicked back. He had a gleaming grin on his tanned face. "Bernie, you missed a tremendous victory," he said. "My soccer team won. And, of course, I was the hero."

Sherman is captain of the soccer team. He plays with his Nyce House buddies, Wes Updood and Joe Sweety.

He grinned his sick, sixty-five-tooth grin at me. "We slaughtered them, one to nothing," he said. "It wasn't even close!"

"Unnnh-huh," I muttered, too tired to talk.

"Want to be jealous? Check out my new soccer

shoes," Sherman said. He stuck his foot in my face. "Feel the leather, Bernie. That's albino pigeon skin. Soft, huh?"

"Grunnnnh," I said.

Sherman pulled a square object from his backpack. He popped it open, and I saw a small video screen.

"This is my new portable DVD recorder and player," he said. "My parents sent it to record all my soccer games, because they're too rich to come watch them in person."

He pushed a few buttons. The soccer game flashed onto the little screen. "Here I am, kicking the winning goal," Sherman said. "I do that every game. That's why we never lose."

Squinting at the screen, I watched Sherman kick the winning goal. Then I watched April-May June and the other cheerleaders run out onto the field. They all hugged Sherman and jumped up and down, and hugged Sherman some more.

I sighed. It is no secret that I have a *major crush* on April-May. I didn't like watching her hug Sherman Oaks.

Sherman saw that I wasn't enjoying it. So he hit rewind and showed it to me again.

"By the way, Bernie," he said, "did *your* team win?"

He burst out laughing. He slapped his knees and tossed back his blond head and laughed and laughed. Then he raised the DVD recorder and *recorded himself* laughing and laughing.

I guess he already knew the answer.

I turned and slumped away, shaking my head.

What's up with this? Sherman Oaks a *winner*? And Bernie Bridges a *loser*?

Something was wrong with this picture.

I had to wipe that grin off Sherman's face. I had to turn the Fighting Apples into winners.

But—how?

Of course I had no idea that The Attack of the Ecch was just days away.

Chapter 5

A NEW CHEER FOR APRIL-MAY

Later that afternoon, I had a study date with my buddies Feenman and Crench. We planned to study some new video games in the Student Center.

I was passing the girls' dorm when April-May June came running out. Her blond hair was tied back in a ponytail. Her blue eyes were the color of the afternoon sky.

She was still wearing her cheerleader outfit: a short-sleeved top and a pleated skirt in our school colors—green, yellow, and purple.

I flashed her my best smile, the one with the

adorable dimples in both cheeks. "April-May, I heard you were looking for me," I said.

She squinted those beautiful eyes at me. "Huh? Excuse me?"

"I heard you wanted me to take you to the Sports Awards Dinner. Now, don't be shy. The answer is yes."

She squinted harder. "Were you tackled on your head?"

I chucked her under the chin. "That's totally sweet," I said. "You're always so shy when I'm around. Shall I pick you up at your dorm an hour before the Awards Dinner?"

"Like you're joking, right?"

I could tell she was nuts about me. What girl can resist the Bernie B. charm when I really turn it on?

"Maybe we could meet after dinner *tonight*," I said. "I could teach you some hot, new cheers. Do you know the one that goes: 'Give me a *B*, give me an *E*, give me an *R*, give me an *N* ...'?"

She rolled her eyes. "Bernie, do you know the cheer that goes: 'Give me an *N*, give me an *O*'?"

"Never heard that one," I said.

My friend Belzer appeared. He handed me a bottle of water. "I know you're thirsty after a big game," he said. "I have six more bottles in my backpack. Are your muscles aching, Bernie? Want me to carry you to the dorm?"

It took a long time to train Belzer. But it was worth it.

"Belzer, not now," I said. "I can't leave April-May. She needs my help with the cheerleader squad."

April-May made a rude spitting noise.

Belzer started to leave. "I'll hang out nearby," he said, "in case you need me to carry you somewhere."

See? He's very well trained.

"April-May," I said, "why don't the cheerleaders come cheer for the football team?"

She stared at me. "Because you're losers?"

"But why only cheer for Sherman and his soccer team?" I asked.

"Because they're winners," she said. "We can't cheer for losers, Bernie. It gets us depressed."

She started to walk away. I tugged her back by her ponytail.

"But what if we win next week?" I said. "Will you

come cheer for my football team?"

She sneered. "Who are you playing next week?" she asked.

"The Ben Franklin Prep School Cannibals."

"Maybe I'll come cheer for you in the hospital," April-May said.

"We could talk about it at dinner tonight," I said.

She flipped her ponytail behind her shoulder. "Sorry, Bernie. I can't have dinner with a loser. How would it look?"

"You're right," I said. "I understand."

I gave her a weak wave. Then I turned and trudged away. The Great Lawn sparkled under the setting sun. But my world was dark. Very dark.

Belzer was waiting under a tree. He held up a towel. "Ready for me to wipe the sweat off your face?"

I didn't have a chance to answer. I heard a thundering sound. The ground shook.

I spun around and saw a big creature bounding toward me across the grass. It didn't take long to realize it was JENNIFER ECCH! And she had her arms outstretched, ready to grab me.

"Run!" Belzer screamed. "Bernie—run!"

Chapter 6

HONEY BUCKET HAS AN IDEA

My shoes pounded the grass as I took off, running full speed across the school grounds. I swerved hard to miss Joe Sweety, one of Sherman's pals.

"Hey, Bernie—how'd that football taste?" he called. "Next time, put some mustard on it. It'll go down easier!"

Ha-ha. I lowered my head and kept running.

I could hear Jennifer Ecch's thundering footsteps close behind me. She was catching up fast. No way I could outrun her.

I call her Nightmare Girl. But that's just being nice.

Jennifer is big and strong. Someone told me she lifts weights *in her sleep*! Yes, she's big and strong and strange. And she's totally in love with me.

How embarrassing is that?

I could see my dorm up ahead. Safety!

But Jennifer was too fast for me. I felt her hot breath on the back of my neck. Then I felt her powerful arms wrap around my waist.

I let out a helpless cry as she tackled me from behind.

I went down hard. I landed on my face. Then the rest of me hit the grass.

I didn't see stars. I didn't see anything. I wondered if I had grass stains on my teeth.

I felt a crushing weight on top of me.

When I opened my eyes, I was sprawled flat on my back and Jennifer was sitting on my chest. "Hi, Bernie," she said. "How's it going?"

"Everything's great," I gasped. "I'm sure I'll start breathing again in a day or so."

She had knitting needles in her hands and a puke-green sweater. "What are you doing?" I choked out. I heard some of my ribs cracking under her weight.

"I'm knitting you a sweater, Sweet Cakes," Jennifer said.

"Please, *please* don't call me Sweet Cakes," I begged.

"Okay, Honey Bucket."

I didn't hear that. Oh, please—tell me I didn't hear her call me that!

"I'm knitting a sweater for you in Ms. Monella's Homemaker class," Jennifer said. She poked me in the side with one of the knitting needles. "I need your help. I need to bring you to class and measure you."

Yikes. Can you think of anything more embarrassing than that?

I must have blacked out for a moment. Jennifer kept talking and poking me with the needle. But her voice faded out. I couldn't hear her.

Suddenly, I woke up. And an awesome idea popped into my head. "Jennifer—do it again!" I cried.

She stared down at me with her one blue eye and one brown eye. "Do what, Sweetie Lamb?"

"Tackle me," I said. "Tackle me again!"

She climbed up and pulled me to my feet. I started to breathe again. It felt good. Breathing is good.

"You want me to tackle you again?" Jennifer asked, scratching her brown bangs with a knitting needle.

I nodded, turned, and took off. I ducked my head into the wind and ran full speed over the grass.

And once again, I heard Jennifer's thundering hoofbeats close in on me. She tackled me hard from behind, and I hit the grass with a loud "Oooof!"

This time I *did* see stars.

Moaning, I climbed to my feet. "Do it again," I said. "Tackle me again."

This time, I didn't run in a straight line. I zigged and zagged, cutting from one side to the other. But Jennifer brought me down in a hard tackle that buried me six inches in the dirt.

Now *everything* hurt. Every part of my body. Even my *shirt* hurt, and it isn't part of me!

This is too dangerous, I decided.

"Belzer—get over here!" I shouted.

He came running. "What can I do for you, Big B?"

"Jennifer," I said. "Tackle Belzer."

Belzer's eyes bulged in his pudgy, round face. He gulped—and took off running. But Belzer didn't stand a chance. He was like a squawking chicken running from a hungry tiger.

Jennifer tackled him easily, pushed him facedown in the dirt, and held him there.

"Again!" I said.

Belzer took off. Jennifer creamed him.

"Again!" I ordered.

I watched Jennifer tackle Belzer again and again. I decided it was time to stop when Belzer couldn't remember his own name.

"Good work!" I said, slapping Belzer on the back. "I'm putting you on the team as Tackling Dummy!"

"Hey! Do you mean it?" Belzer cried happily. "Wow! I made the team!"

Belzer wobbled off, staggering in crazy zigzags. He was still dazed. I watched him walk straight into Pooper's Pond. Some kids had to fish him out.

I turned to Jennifer. "I'm a genius! You are going to turn the Apples into *Killers*!"

Jennifer closed her blue eye and squinted at me with the brown eye. "But, Honey Bucket—what about my sweater?"

I grinned at her. "Jennifer, when the Apples win the State Championship, I'll let you knit me TEN sweaters!"

Chapter 7

ADVICE FROM COACH BUNZ

I was excited. I knew I had a secret weapon that would turn our football team into champions. The next afternoon, I hurried to the gym to tell Coach Bunz about it.

I found him at the sink in the locker room. He was dipping silver whistles one by one into the water.

He greeted me with a nod. "I like to wet my whistle."

Did that make any sense? I don't think so.

"Preparation," Coach Bunz said. "That's the key,

Bernie. Always be prepared. Don't put your underwear on backwards, and keep your whistle wet."

"I'll remember that, Coach," I said. "Words of wisdom."

"Always give it a hundred and ten percent," Coach Bunz said. "Know what I'm saying? If you don't come to play, how do you expect to play?" He dipped another whistle into the sink.

"Good thinking, sir," I said. "I'm going to write this advice down as soon as I get back to my room. But I want to tell you—"

"Take it one game at a time," he said. "And focus. Remember to focus." He took the whistle out of the sink and blew it. It sent up a spray of water.

"Bernie, keep your head down," he said. "Remember to keep your feet moving and bend your knees."

"Thank you, sir," I said. "I'll pass that along to the guys. But I really want to tell you—"

"What's your angle, Bernie?" His big belly turned away from the sink. A few seconds later, *he* turned away from the sink. "I'm very surprised you like to play football."

"Surprised, sir?"

He nodded. "I know you pay Belzer to go to gym class in your place," he said.

"Oh, no," I said. "Belzer goes gladly, sir. I don't have to pay. Maybe only a few dollars. He wants to be a gym teacher like you. It's his *dream* to wear a sweaty sweatshirt and a whistle."

"Level with me, Bridges," Coach Bunz said. "Why do you want to play football? Why are you on this team?"

No way I could tell him the truth.

I tried out for the football team because I wanted to grind Sherman Oaks into the mud. What better reason could there be?

There he was, winning soccer game after soccer game. Sherman was so stuck-up now, he had the word SUPERSTAR stenciled on his butt! The cheerleaders were going nuts for him. The whole school was talking about him.

Could Bernie B. stand for that? Of course not.

That's why I signed up to lead the football team. But I couldn't tell Coach Bunz that.

"I'm only interested in winning for my school,

sir," I said. "I live for football! Rah rah rah!"

"Good answer," Coach Bunz said. "But what's your angle, Bridges? Don't you want to sell popcorn and souvenirs and cash in on the team?"

I gasped. "Sell popcorn? Souvenirs? Cash in? Me, sir? That's not like me at all."

Good idea, I thought. *We'll get to work on that tonight!*

"I want to tell you my new plan, sir," I started to say.

"Keep your shoulder pads down," the coach said. "And hold on to the ball. Ball control. Let them know you've come to play. But don't run into the pile. Follow your blocking, Bernie."

"Okay, sir, but—"

He blew another whistle. It sprayed water in his face.

"These whistles are ruined," he muttered. "They don't work at all." He tossed them in the trash and stomped away.

Chapter 8

A GREAT PEP TALK

Game time Saturday afternoon. I watched the Ben Franklin Prep School Cannibals come piling out of their school bus. They looked big and mean.

It was easy to see how *psyched* they were for the game. They were *biting* one another!

A grin spread over my handsome face. *No problem,* I told myself. I have a secret weapon. They may arrive here as Cannibals, but they're going home as Clowns!

In the locker room, my teammates were getting suited up for the game. Crench was trying to pull his shoulder pads up over his legs.

"What's wrong with you?" I demanded. The poor guy was so scared, he was trembling.

"Bernie, did you see their team?" he asked, grabbing my arm. "These guys are tough, Bernie. They're in fourth grade, right? But they've all got *mustaches*!"

"No problem," I said.

"Look at their warm-up exercises," Feenman said. "They throw each other over the goalposts!"

"No problem," I said.

"Hey, look who's in the locker room," Crench said, pointing. "It's Headmaster Upchuck!"

"Problem," I said.

Headmaster Upchuck *never* visits our locker room. He doesn't like kids. He thinks we smell bad. And we make him tense. So he usually hides all day in his office.

He's a very short, little man. He's shorter than a lot of the fourth graders.

His head is bald and kinda shaped like a football. No matter what is happening, he always wears the same baggy gray suit. We think it's glued on.

What did he want?

Our cleats clanked on the floor as we all lined up

to greet him. "You're looking good, sir," I said cheerfully. "That gray color really looks good on you. It matches your skin."

He started to tremble. He always shakes a lot when he sees me coming. "Bernie, please—" he said.

"I like that suit," I said. "You know, I've seen that suit on TV!"

"Really?" the Headmaster said.

"It was on a ventriloquist's dummy," I said. "But it looks much better on *you*, sir!"

"Bernie, step back and let the Headmaster speak," Coach Bunz said. He bumped me out of the way with his stomach.

Coach Bunz turned to my teammates. "The Headmaster has made a special surprise visit to our locker room to speak to you boys," he said. He slid his hands under the Headmaster's armpits and lifted him off the floor so we could all see him.

"That won't be necessary," Upchuck said. "Put me down."

Back on the floor, Upchuck cleared his throat loudly. "I've come to give you Fighting Apples a pep talk!" he said in his high, shrill voice.

"I know that you players have *greatness* hidden somewhere deep inside you!" Upchuck said. "I'm so proud of you boys. You may *play* like pitiful losers. But I know that deep inside . . . you're uh . . . something something. Yada yada yada."

He stopped. We stared at him in silence, waiting for him to continue the pep talk.

"That's it," Upchuck said. "That's my pep talk. Go out there, boys, and do your best not to embarrass the school like total jerks!"

"Great pep talk!" Coach Bunz said. "Let's hear it for Headmaster Upchuck!"

We all cheered and clapped.

The Headmaster turned to Coach Bunz. "Who is the captain of this team?" he asked.

"Bernie Bridges," Coach Bunz replied.

The Headmaster's face went white as flour. His lips trembled. "Oh. Forget the whole thing!" he cried.

He turned and stomped out of the locker room. His tiny shoes didn't make a sound.

I guess Headmaster Upchuck didn't have any faith in me. But I didn't care.

I knew that everyone was in for a BIG surprise.

44

Chapter 9

THE SECRET WEAPON

The first half of our game against the Ben Franklin Cannibals was a tremendous victory for my team. We were only losing 45 to 6.

Feenman and Crench dropped about thirty passes—even with their helmets turned the right way. "What's wrong with my passes?" I asked them.

"Bernie," Feenman said, "you keep hitting me in the hands!"

And our best running back—Mason Dixon—ran the wrong way twice and scored two touchdowns for the other team.

"Good game, guys! Good game!" I shouted as they carried me off the field on their shoulders for halftime.

I wasn't worried. I knew my secret weapon was ready to go.

When the second half started, I brought her out.

You should have heard the shouts and cries of disbelief as Jennifer Ecch came trotting onto the field, her helmet perched on her head. Her big cleats kicked up clouds of dust as she ran.

"A GIRL? A girl can't play!" one of the Cannibals shouted.

"Is this a joke?" another Cannibal cried.

"Get her off the field! NO GIRLS!"

The Cannibals were going nuts. I knew why they were upset. Jennifer was bigger than anyone on the field. Bigger and wider and stronger.

She and I had practiced a Mean Face expression. We'd practiced it in front of a mirror for hours. I told her she had to use the Mean Face. It was part of the game.

Now she turned and gave the Cannibals the Mean Face. Brown eye up, blue eye down, teeth bared in a nasty, furious dog snarl.

Scary!

It scared *me*—and I knew she was on my side! And now I could see the looks of fear in the eyes of the Cannibals.

And I knew what they were thinking: Her HEAD was bigger than the football!

"No girls! No girls! No girls!" they all started to chant.

"Give her a chance! Give her a chance! Give her a chance!" I started a cheer with *my* team.

On the sidelines, I saw Coach Bunz shaking his head. This was a surprise to him, too.

Jennifer snarled at the other team. "Where do I stand, Honey Cakes?" she asked.

"Don't call me Honey Cakes!" I screamed. "You don't say the words 'Honey Cakes' on a football field."

The whistle blew. The game was starting. The Cannibals had the ball.

"Here. Stand over here." I tugged Jennifer into place.

She hugged me. "This is so exciting!" she cried.

I could hear a lot of guys laughing at me.

"No hugging," I said, pushing her back. "I told you to read the rule book. No hugging. It says that on page four."

The linemen locked into place. The play was about to begin.

"Jennifer, face the front!" I shouted. "You're looking the wrong way."

"Sorry, Honey Breath. I was looking at *you*."

Oh, wow. Maybe this was a big mistake. I crossed all my fingers.

"Get ready," I told her. "You're the middle linebacker."

She blinked. "What does that mean?"

"Tackle anything that moves!" I cried.

Chapter 10

ATTACK OF THE ECCH

The play started. The Cannibal runner came crashing toward us.

I started to move—*and Jennifer tackled ME!*

I hit the ground hard. She landed on top of me. The Cannibal runner shot right past us.

"How did I do?" Jennifer asked, pulling me to my feet.

I groaned. "You got it wrong!" I cried. "The other team! You tackle someone from the *other team!*"

"Why didn't you say so?" She gave me a shove that sent me toppling into Crench.

"Your girlfriend has some problems with the rules," Crench said.

"She's *not* my girlfriend," I said. "And she's going to be an awesome football player."

"Sweet Cakes, tell me where to stand again!" Jennifer shouted, loud enough for everyone on the field to hear.

I lined her up. "Now remember," I said. "Tackle someone from the *other* team."

"I get it." She leaned forward and pawed the ground, eager for the play to start.

Another running play. The Cannibal fullback came bursting toward us with his helmet lowered.

"YAAAAAII!" Jennifer let out a terrifying battle cry. Then she tackled him. She tackled him so hard, she buried him two feet in the ground.

The two officials signaled frantically to the coaches. They came running onto the field carrying shovels. And they dug the Cannibal runner out of the ground.

"Was that good?" Jennifer asked.

"Not bad," I said.

The next Cannibal play was a pass play. The

receiver caught the ball. But Jennifer was there. She tackled him so hard, we could all hear his teeth rattle.

The ball fell loose. Jennifer picked it up and turned to me. "Which way do I go?"

I pointed.

She took off. She ran right over several players and both officials. She left big footprints on their backs! She ran for a touchdown—and kept running.

"Stop! Stop!" We all ran after her. "Jennifer—stop!"

She was halfway across the Great Lawn, almost to Pooper's Pond. What did she plan to do? Slam-dunk the ball in the water?

Feenman and Crench pulled her back on the field.

"Jennifer—you scored a touchdown!" I told her.

She brushed her bangs out of her eyes and grinned. "I'm starting to like this game," she said.

Some of the Cannibal players were still picking themselves up off the ground. It took a while to get things started again.

When the game finally continued, everyone could see that the Cannibals didn't stand a chance. My secret weapon exploded all over the field. Jennifer ran and tackled and *creamed* everyone in her path.

The Fighting Apples won the game by twenty-one points.

Can you imagine the excitement?

Our school is a hundred years old. And this was the *first* football game we'd ever won! We'd lost

1,500 straight games. But the losing streak had finally ended.

The players were so happy, we tried to carry Jennifer off the field on our shoulders. But we couldn't lift her. So Jennifer carried *me* off the field. Then we all jumped in the air and screamed at the top of our lungs.

Coach Bunz came rumbling over to us, his stomach bouncing in front of him. He had a big smile on his face.

"Way to go!" he told Jennifer. He slapped her on the back. He shouldn't have done that. He broke several fingers.

"I'm glad you like my secret weapon, sir," I said. "I don't want to take *all* the credit for the win. But I think I made the right choice here. Of course, I'll share the credit with Jennifer. I mean, she had something to do with our win, too."

Coach Bunz ignored me. He walked off with Jennifer. "You've got to play to win," he told her. "Showing up is the most important thing. Hit the line hard. You've got to see the whole field at once. It's a team game. Contribute. Just focus and contribute."

Jennifer turned back to me. "What is he talking about?" she asked.

I shrugged. "Beats me. But the man really knows his football."

Laughing and cheering, my teammates trotted into the locker room. Jennifer came running up to me. "Bernie, that was so *exciting*!" she gushed. She grabbed my hand and started to plant smoochy kisses all over it.

"Down, girl, down!" I cried.

I pulled my hand free and wiped it dry on my shirt. "No smoochy hand kissing. That's on page twenty-three. Didn't you read the rule book?"

She smiled at me. "Remember, Sweet Knees, you promised if we win the championship, you'll come to my Homemaker class? And you'll let me measure you for ten sweaters?"

Ha-ha. Win the championship? Fat chance! We just won our *first game in one hundred years! Forget about the championship*, I thought. *That's science fiction!*

"Know what I'm going to put on each sweater?" Jennifer asked, pinching my cheek. "They're all going to say 'Bernie Loves Jen' inside a big red heart. Nice?"

"Nice," I said. Ha-ha. Fat chance.

"Tell you what," I told her. "If we win the State Championship, I'll help you pick out the yarn! Then I'll model all ten sweaters in front of the whole school!"

Chapter 11

BIG NEWS FROM APRIL-MAY

On Saturday, we played the Mercy Academy Mad Dogs. They looked terrifying—and some of them actually foamed at the mouth.

I knew we didn't stand a chance.

Before the game, Feenman and Crench helped me pad my uniform with big slabs of foam rubber. The foam rubber made it hard to walk or move my arms. But at least when I hit the dirt, I wouldn't feel it.

My teammates didn't want Bernie B. to feel any pain.

To my surprise, a crowd showed up on the field to watch the game. "Go, Jennifer!" I heard a girl shout.

And I heard two other kids chanting, "Ecch! Ecch! Ecch!"

Weird. Were they cheering for Jennifer? Or did they have something stuck in their throats?

Well, we gave them something to shout about.

Jennifer stampeded over the Mad Dogs like a . . . like a mad dog! She still didn't understand the rules. She ran in every direction and tackled anyone who came near. In the second quarter, I saw her tackle a *tree*!

Beast showed Jennifer how to head-butt—his favorite move—and she started head-butting everyone in sight! Then she and Beast started head-butting each other. We had to pull them apart so the game could continue.

I tossed Jennifer a pass. She didn't know what to do with it. So she head-butted the ball to Feenman—and he ran for a touchdown! "I like this!" Feenman shouted.

Suddenly we were acting like a team! Beast stopped grazing on the grass long enough to block.

Feenman and Crench didn't want to look bad in front of a girl, so they started catching my passes. Even I ran for a touchdown, with Jennifer head-butting everyone in my path.

We won 45 to 0.

The Rotten School crowd went wild, leaping in the air and shouting, "Ecch! Ecch! Ecch!" The cheer rolled over the field.

The Mad Dogs slumped back onto their school bus, whimpering and trembling.

Two victories in a row. Am I a football genius or what?

Later, I was walking across the Great Lawn, feeling awesome, making up some cheers about *me*— when Sherman Oaks appeared.

"Dude, I just won my soccer game," he said. "We slaughtered them two to nothing."

I started to tell him about my football game. But he pushed a ball into my face. "Check out my new soccer ball."

He rubbed it over my nose and forehead. "Go

ahead—feel it, Bernie. Soft, huh? It's made out of grebe skin."

I squinted at the ball. "Sherman, what's a grebe?"

He shrugged. "I don't know. Some kind of grebe, I guess."

"Did you kick the winning goal with it?" I asked.

"No way," Sherman said. "I wouldn't kick this ball. It's too valuable! I keep it in my safe."

Sherman is the only fourth grader I know who has a *wall safe* in his room.

He pulled out his portable DVD player. "Let me show you the game highlights," he said. "Of course, I'm in all of them."

But before he could start the DVD player, April-May June came running up. She was in her green, yellow, and purple cheerleading uniform. Her blond hair floated behind her as she ran.

"Bernie—I've got big news!" she cried breathlessly.

Chapter 12

WHAT RHYMES WITH ECCH?

Sherman's eyes grew wide. "Big news about my soccer game?" he asked April-May. "You want a highlight reel? I'll be happy to make a copy and e-mail you all my best plays."

"It's not about you," April-May said sharply.

He gasped in shock and nearly dropped his grebe ball.

She turned her back on Sherman and flashed me a smile. "It's about *your* team, Bernie," she said.

"My team?" I said. "Well, yes, I've whipped that team into shape. I know we have a long way to go.

But they're starting to listen to me. And it shows!"

April-May kept her awesome smile on me. Sunshine. *Sunshine!* Her smile was so bright, I had to hide my eyes.

"Bernie," she said, "the cheerleaders have decided that—now that you're not pitiful, geeky losers—we are going to come cheer for *your* games!"

Sherman gasped again. "But—but—what about my soccer games?" he sputtered.

"You don't need us anymore," April-May snapped. "The football team is a lot more exciting." She tossed her hair over her shoulder. "Especially since Bernie put Jennifer Ecch on the team."

April-May shook my hand. "Bernie, I'm so *proud* of you for letting a girl play."

"Yes, I'm a pioneer," I said. "And I'm proud of it. I really think girls are almost as good as boys in sports. I think we need even *more* girls on the football team."

I grinned at Sherman. "I think girls should be on *all* teams—even soccer teams!"

Sherman choked.

I slapped him hard on the back until he started breathing normal again.

"Bernie," April-May said, "if the Apples win the football championship, I'll have lunch with you in the Dining Hall!" Then she added, "If you promise to eat fast."

My heart leaped around in my chest.

"Yes! Of course, I eat fast," I said. "Of course, we'll win the championship."

I flashed her my best dimpled grin. "Especially with *you* and the other cheerleaders there to cheer us on!"

She seemed to like that.

"Here's a new cheer you might want to try," I said. I stepped back and performed it for her, jumping and waving my arms in the air.

"Give me a *B*! Give me an *E*! Give me an *R*! Give me an *N*! Give me a—"

Sherman shoved his finger down his throat. "Give me a *P-U-K-E*!" He groaned.

"Here's the new cheer *I've* been working on," April-May said.

She put her hands on her waist, tossed back her head, and shouted at the top of her lungs. "Give me an ECCH! Give me an ECCH! Give me an ECCH ECCH ECCH!"

She did a perfect cartwheel. "Bernie, the cheer isn't quite finished. What rhymes with Ecch?"

I thought hard. "Blecch?"

She frowned. "It still needs work."

Sherman pulled out his wallet. He took out a hundred-dollar bill and waved it in April-May's face.

"I'm a generous dude. I'll pay the cheerleaders one hundred dollars to cheer at the soccer games," he said.

April-May gasped. "Sherman! Are you trying to bribe a *cheerleader?*" she cried. "Don't you know you can't bribe a cheerleader!"

I grabbed the bill from his hand. "Sherman, what's wrong with you?" I scolded. "It's not about money. It's about school spirit. It's about the joy of winning for our wonderful Rotten School!"

"Bernie is right," April-May said.

I folded up the money and jammed it into my pocket. "I'll see that this goes to a good charity," I said. "I'll donate it to The Bernie Bridges Marshmallow-Ripple Banana Ice Cream After-Dinner Fund."

"I have to go work on my cheer," April-May said. "I know *something* rhymes with Ecch."

She did another perfect cartwheel, just to show off. Then she took off, heading toward the girls' dorm.

I felt like doing a cartwheel, too.

Sherman, on the other hand, didn't look too

happy. His face was bright red, and he was gritting his teeth.

He gripped the soccer ball between his hands. And he squeezed it so hard, he popped his grebe ball!

Angrily, he tossed it to the ground, turned, and strode away.

Well, well. Everything was going Bernie B.'s way today. Everything was going great.

I shut my eyes and pictured myself winning the football championship ... being carried off the field with all the cheerleaders shouting my name ... sitting in the Dining Hall ... chatting over lunch with April-May June.

Dream on, Bernie. Dream on.

I should have known that Sherman would find a way to mess things up....

Chapter 13

SHERMAN'S EVIL PLOT

My guys and I had a big celebration that night in Rotten House, our dorm. Thanks to Sherman's hundred-dollar bill, we had tons and tons of marshmallow-ripple banana ice cream to celebrate with.

We didn't bother scooping it into bowls. We each had our own gallon! Feenman and Crench ate it with their hands. Beast had his head buried in the carton. When he finished the ice cream, he swallowed the box.

Okay, maybe we overdid it with the marshmallow-ripple. Late that night, I was awakened by loud noises from down the hall.

RRRRRRAAAAAGGGGGGH

URRRRRRRGGGGGH

NUURRRRRRRRRGGH

No mistaking it. I'd heard it before. Guys in the third-floor bathroom, barfing their brains out.

"Hey, dudes!" I sat up in bed and shouted. "Could you barf to yourselves? I need my sleep, remember? Big game on Saturday!"

rrrrrraagggggghhhh

urrrrrrrrrrgggggh

nurrrrrrgggggghnnnn

69

Good guys. Much quieter. I could tell they were covering their mouths as they hurled.

The next afternoon, I was still joyful, still floating on my victory, still gleefully innocent of what was waiting for me.

But I stopped when I got to the practice field.

Feenman and Crench came hurrying over. Feenman shook his head. "We've got a problem, Big B."

They both pointed to the crowd in the center of the field.

"Girls!" Crench cried. "At least a dozen, Bernie. Maybe more."

"They came to watch us practice?" I asked.

"They came to play," Crench replied.

"Huh? Play *what*?" I cried. "You don't mean..."

I jogged up to the crowd of girls. I recognized Flora and Fauna, the Peevish twins—friends of Sherman's. And I saw April-May's good friend Sharonda Davis. And lots of other girls, all talking at once.

"Hey, good to see you!" I said cheerfully. "You

girls getting some sun? Hope you remembered your suntan lotion. If you need any, I have some tubes for sale. Only two dollars each."

I motioned to the sidelines. "Sunbathers over there, please. Make room for the team to practice."

"Bernie, we came to play," Flora said.

The other girls all nodded and cheered and jumped up and down excitedly.

"You came to play volleyball?" I said. "Sorry. We don't have a net. Have you tried the gym?"

Sharonda Davis stepped up to me. Sharonda is a tall, lanky girl with an attitude. "Volleyball? You're joking, right? Bernie, we came to play on the football team."

"You go, girl!" her friends shouted.

Sharonda poked me in the stomach with a football. Just to show me who's boss, I guess. "Sherman said you are *desperate* for more girls on your team. So here we are." She said each word with a poke in the stomach.

"Sherman?" I cried, my voice cracking. "*Sherman* said *what?!*"

And suddenly I realized what was happening here.

This was Sherman's plot against me. He sends over a bunch of girls who have *no clue* how to play football. So I lose all my games. And the cheerleaders go back to the soccer team. And Sherman is the big, shining star once again.

I got Sherman's plot. I got it, okay.

But what could I *do* about it?

I had to send them away. If I let these girls on the

team, we'd be total losers again.

I had to be strong. I had to be brave.

"Sorry, girls," I started. "I hate to disappoint you, but I'm afraid—"

And then I saw April-May June watching from the sidelines. Watching and listening.

"Uh ... I hate to disappoint you," I said, "but I'm afraid your uniforms won't be ready until Friday!"

Chapter 14

AM I DOOMED OR AM I DOOMED?

Don't get me wrong. I know girls can be really good athletes. But these girls didn't understand the game.

"I want to kick a touchdown!" Flora shouted at practice.

Her sister, Fauna, caught a long pass after it bounced once. "Hey, I caught it!" she shouted. "How many points is that?"

"How many points for running out-of-bounds?" one of them shouted.

It was not an easy week for the team leader, Bernie B. And Coach Bunz was no help at all. He just kept shouting, "Focus! Focus! Bend but don't break! Keep your whistle wet!"

No one knew what the heck he was talking about!

To make matters worse, Jennifer Ecch showed up at practice loaded down with big balls of wool. She kept holding them up to my face one at a time.

"This color is a little too pale," she'd say. "This color is too bright. This one brings out your eyes, but it may be too scratchy. What do you think, Bernie?"

"Jennifer, they're all perfect," I said. "Use them all. I'll be a rainbow!"

She squealed with happiness.

"Jennifer, please—no squealing!" I said. "Rules! Rules!"

I knew there was no way we'd win the championship now. The good news: Jennifer would *not* be knitting any sweaters for me. The bad news: No way I'd be having lunch with April-May.

An hour before our game with the Jimmy Neutron Academy Maniacs, April-May came running up to me in her cheerleader uniform. "Go, Bernie!" she cheered. "Go, Bernie! Go, Bernie!"

"April-May, I like that new cheer," I said. "Did you make that up by yourself?"

"We all worked on it," April-May replied. "We cheerleaders are totally *thrilled* you put so many girls on the team."

"We needed the balance," I said. "Before, we had too many kids who knew how to play. Now, we've fixed that."

"Go, Bernie!" she cried. She backflipped over to the other cheerleaders on the sidelines.

My stomach suddenly did some backflips of its own.

I'm doomed, I thought. *Sherman really got me this time. We're going to be* slaughtered! *And Sherman's soccer team will probably win the State Championship.*

And then I watched the Maniacs climb down from their school bus. They piled off, grunting and head-butting one another. They were all as big as rhinoceroses! Some of them even had single *horns* growing out of their foreheads!

I turned and saw Jennifer Ecch watching from the field. Jennifer Ecch, our secret weapon. And even *she* was trembling, her whole body shaking and quaking, her teeth chattering.

Doomed, I thought. The Fighting Apples will be applesauce in an hour. Totally doomed.

A whistle blew. The game was starting.

Flora and Fauna came running up to me. "It's our first game," Flora said. "Give us a pep talk, Bernie. You're the team leader!"

"Yeah. Give us a pep talk," Fauna said.

The whole team huddled together on the side of the field.

"A pep talk? Okay," I said. "Pep talk. Pep talk. Let me see. . . . Does everyone know where we keep the first-aid kit?"

Chapter 15

How to Beat Maniacs

I glanced over to the other side of the field. The Maniacs were grunting and growling, still head-butting one another, locking horns, waiting for us to come play.

I looked for my buddies Feenman and Crench. I spotted them hiding behind Coach Bunz. Cowards!

Okay. Pain time. I took a deep breath. "Let's go out there and show these guys what *Rotten* means!" I shouted. I clapped my hands and went running onto the field, leading my team to the slaughter.

I saw Sherman standing with his arms crossed in

front of him. He had a big, gloating grin on his face. He flashed me a thumbs-up and started to laugh.

And that's when I had a brilliant idea.

Bernie B., you're a genius! In all modesty, a *genius*!

The whistle blew. The game started. The Apples had the ball first.

I called my team into a huddle. All girls—and me. And I knew I couldn't lose!

"You girls all line up in front," I told them. "Jennifer and I will stay in the backfield." I clapped my hands. "Let's get 'em!"

"But what's the play?" Flora asked.

"Don't worry about a play," I said. "Just take off your helmets. When you get to the line, take off your helmets."

Jennifer and I hung back. "Honey Cakes, what's up with the no helmets?" Jennifer asked.

"Just watch," I said.

The girls trotted up to face the Maniacs and pulled off their helmets. They shook out their hair.

"Hey! It's GIRLS!" a Maniac linebacker shouted.

"Yo! We didn't come here to play a bunch of girls!" another Maniac cried.

"You gotta be kidding!" A big lineman groaned.
"Girls? Playing football? It's a joke—right?"

"We're just as good as you," Flora Peevish said.
She stuck out her tongue.

"This is *sick!*" a Maniac shouted. "Where's the REAL team? We can't play girls!"

Flora gave him a shove. He shoved her back. Her sister, Fauna, shoved another player. He pulled her hair.

While they all argued, I handed the ball to Jennifer and she *walked* across the field, into the end zone for a touchdown. No one touched her. No one on the other team even *saw* her!

We kicked the extra point. Seven to nothing, Fighting Apples.

On the sidelines, April-May and the cheerleaders were going wild. "Ecch! Ecch! Ecch!" they cheered. "We don't know what it rhymes with! Ecch! Ecch! Ecch!"

Sherman had an unhappy frown on his face.

Now the Maniacs had the ball. I sent the same girls back on the field with Jennifer and Beast.

"What do we do?" Sharonda asked. "Try to tackle them?"

"No way," I said. "Don't worry about tackling. How many of you girls are in the choir?" I asked.

They all raised their hands.

"When the play starts, sing that hymn you sing every morning," I told them.

They trotted up to the line. The Maniac quarterback yelled, "Hike!" and took the ball from his center.

The girls began to sing their hymn. I'd never heard such beautiful voices.

The Maniacs all stopped. They were staring at one another, shrugging their shoulder pads. Totally confused.

Beast head-butted the quarterback right in the stomach. Jennifer grabbed the ball and ran for another touchdown.

We kicked the extra point just as the girls finished their hymn. It was beautiful. Not a dry eye on the field.

And the score: Apples 14, Maniacs zippo.

See? Football is all about strategy. And who knows strategy better than Bernie B.?

Flora, Fauna, and the other girls gathered around me. "This is fun!" Fauna cried. "What's our next play, Bernie?"

"How many of you girls can do cartwheels?" I asked.

Chapter 16

SHERMAN FEELS SORRY

Belzer brought me breakfast in bed the next morning. Good kid, Belzer.

Feenman and Crench must have smelled the eggs and bacon from their room across the hall. They came loping in, sniffing the air like dogs.

"Good game yesterday!" Feenman said, grabbing a slice of bacon off my plate. "Fifty-two to nothing. Those girls can really play football!"

"I just called the right plays," I said. "No big deal."

"Let's hear it for Bernie!" Belzer cried.

We all cheered and punched knuckles and did

the secret Rotten School Handshake.

I stabbed Crench with my fork when he made a grab for my biscuits. "Who is our next victim?" I asked.

"The Pushnik Country Day School Pushovers," Crench said.

We all laughed.

"They're pitiful losers," Feenman said, eating my fruit cocktail with his hands. "We'll win by at least a hundred points."

Belzer was ironing my school blazer for me. He shook his head. "Bernie, if the Apples win, you'll have to let The Ecch knit ten sweaters for you. And they will all have hearts on them, saying, 'Bernie Loves Jen.'"

"I don't care," I said. "April-May came to me after the game yesterday. She said if we win the next game, she'll let me sit at her table in the Dining Hall for an entire week!"

Feenman pumped his fists in the air. "We're going to be the state champs!" he shouted.

"You're a hero, Big B!" Belzer cried.

We all cheered and did the secret handshake

again. I looked down at my tray. Feenman and Crench had eaten my entire breakfast!

Skip ahead fifteen minutes. I was shuffling across the Great Lawn, on my way to class. A bright, sunny morning—until Sherman Oaks appeared.

"Like my new soccer shirt?" he asked, stepping in front of me. "It's made out of my own hair! That's why it's so soft and beautiful."

"Sweet," I muttered. I tried to move around him, but he blocked my path.

Sherman put a hand on my shoulder. "I feel terrible about your game next Saturday," he said. "I really do."

"Against the Pushovers?" I said. "We're gonna win big-time."

"I know," Sherman said, shaking his head sadly. "That's why I feel sorry for you."

I stared at him. "Sorry for me? What do you mean?"

Chapter 17

HUGE BOYS

Sherman raised his DVD player and pushed some buttons. On the screen came the biggest, meanest, ugliest fourth-grade football team I'd ever seen.

"Sherman, what is this?" I asked, staring at the faces on the screen. "You're showing me zoo animals? Can these huge beasts survive in captivity?"

"If you beat the Pushovers on Saturday," Sherman said, "*this* is the team you play for the State Championship."

"Who—who *are* they?" I stammered.

"It's the team from the Huge Boys Academy,"

Sherman said. "Know what their team name is? The Bone-Breakers!"

I watched the team playing on the DVD screen. "What's that cracking sound?" I asked.

"They're breaking bones," Sherman said. "That's what they do. They like to break bones."

Craaaaaak.
Craaaaaaaak.

"Sherman, turn that thing off!" I cried. "We can't play a team that big! We—we—" My chin hit the ground.

"You'll *have* to play them," Sherman said, a big grin on his face. "You'll have to play the Bone-Breakers, Bernie—if you beat the Pushovers!"

I walked away, shaking my head. The sun was still bright and warm, but I saw only darkness. And I felt a chill that ran down my whole body.

We've got to LOSE on Saturday! I told myself. *I can't allow the team to win.*

We've got to LOSE! But ...*how?*

Chapter 18

THE NEW ALL-STARS

A whole new team. That was the answer. My team was too good. I had to put together a team so *lame*, it would lose to the pitiful Pushovers.

I rounded up guys from my dorm. I knew my buddies would come through for me—and help us lose big-time on Saturday.

That afternoon, I dragged them out to the practice field.

"Nosebleed, get over here," I said. "Go out for a pass."

"But, Bernie," he whined. "It's too windy out

here. You know a strong wind gives me a nosebleed."

"That's why you're the new wide receiver," I said. "Here. Catch." I started to heave the ball to him.

"Time out! Time out!" he shouted. "I've got a nosebleed!" He went running to the locker room for tissues.

"Who's next?" I called. "Chipmunk! Line up!"

Chipmunk is the shyest, most timid guy in school. He's so bashful, he burps into his *shirt pocket*!

"Chipmunk, you're the new middle linebacker," I said. "Tackle anyone who comes at you."

He gulped. "Tackle? Do I have to *touch* them?"

"You go, dude! You'll be an all-star!" I cried.

He lowered his head and blushed bright red.

Next, I made Billy the Brain a running back. Billy is the brainiest guy at the Rotten School. He's so smart, he can read the funny pages in the newspaper in less than an hour! But he's never played sports in his life.

"Bernie," he said, "did you know that baseball was invented by Tom Cruise in 1927? I saw it in a movie."

"Brilliant!" I said.

"And did you know there are no flies in a fly ball?"

"Brilliant! You're our new running back!"

"Football is all a matter of geometry," Billy the Brain said. "Once I figure out the hypotenuse, I'll have it made."

"You go, dude!" I shouted.

And then I had my *best*, most *awesome* idea. I turned to Feenman and Crench. "See that new kid walking on the path? What's his name? Farley Mopes? Bring him over here."

Feenman stared at me. "But, Bernie—he's blind!"

"Are you prejudiced?" I demanded.

"No, but—"

"Bring him over here. I like the looks of this dude."

He was a big kid, almost popping out of his school blazer. He had straight, brown hair falling over his face. Feenman brought him across the field to me.

"How about playing football on Saturday?" I asked him. "I want you on my team."

Farley's mouth dropped open. "But I'm *blind!*" he cried.

"We're all equal around here," I said. I shoved the ball into his hands. "I believe in giving *everyone* a chance. You're the new quarterback!"

"No—wait!" He said. "I'm blind! Didn't you hear me? I'm blind!"

Feenman led him into the huddle.

The team was set. I watched them stumble around the field.

Nosebleed was bleeding on the bench. Billy the Brain was holding a calculator, trying to figure out the hypotenuse. Chipmunk was hiding behind the Power Juice bucket. Farley Mopes was facing the wrong way!

"Sweet!" I cried. "Bernie, you've done it again! We can't win on Saturday! We *can't*!"

Chapter 19

THE ECCH PROBLEM

I had one more big problem. The Ecch Problem.

If Jennifer played, we still had a chance of winning. I *had* to find a way to keep her out of the game.

I met her Friday afternoon at the Fitness Center. She was on her back, lifting 300-pound weights—with one hand!

"Sweet Cakes!" she cried when she saw me.

Everyone in the gym turned to stare at us.

"Do you have to call me that?" I whispered. "Please don't call me that."

"It's just a cute nickname," she said. "You don't

really think it's too icky-poo, do you?"

Icky-poo?

She grabbed my blazer sleeve and used it to wipe all the sweat off her face and neck. Then she pulled herself up from the weight machine. "Bernie, did you come to discuss plans for the game here tomorrow?"

"Kinda," I said. "Coach Bunz was talking to me," I lied. "He needs a new bench captain for tomorrow. I told him you'd be perfect."

She squinted at me with her brown eye. "Bench captain? Me?"

"You've worked hard. You've earned it," I said. I shook her hand. "Congratulations, Jennifer. Only your third game, and you've made captain!"

"But—" Now she squinted at me with her blue eye. "Does that mean I stay on the bench?"

"Of course," I said. "You must be so *proud*! You're the captain. It's awesome! You control everything! Who sits, who stands, who gets a towel ... all up to you!"

She squinted at me with *both* eyes. "Hmmm ..."

I pulled out my cell phone. "Here. Use this to call

your parents and tell them the big news. Their daughter is a *captain!*"

She shook her head. "I don't think so," she said. "The team needs me too much."

I swallowed. "The team needs you on the bench!" I insisted. "Someone has to guard the Power Juice and the paper cups!"

"Sorry, Bernie. It's a real honor, but I have to turn it down. I owe it to the team to play."

Strike one. That try didn't work. Now the sweat was pouring down *my* forehead. I had only one more idea. It *had* to work.

"Okay, okay," I said. "Forget the bench captain thing. I'll tell you the truth. I'm worried about your hands."

She gasped. "My hands? What about my hands?" She held them up. They were as big as boxing gloves!

"Look at them," I said. "Swollen from playing too many football games. I'm worried about my sweaters, Jen. If anything happens to your precious hands during the game, you won't be able to knit my ten sweaters. And ... and ... I'll be crushed."

"Oh, Bernie!" she cried. She wrapped me in a hug. I heard at least forty ribs crack.

"You're right!" she said. "I had no *clue* the sweaters were so important to you. I can't let anything happen to my knitting hands. I'll do as you say. I'll stay on the bench this week!"

Success! I let out a long sigh. "Thank you! Thank you!" I cried.

She grabbed my hand and began planting smoochy kisses on it, first one side, then the other.

I didn't care. The game was in the bag. *No way* we'd win now!

Chapter 20

DOOMED

Saturday afternoon. A cloudy, gray day. But I felt sunny inside. I was watching my team—the Fighting Apples—get pushed over by the Pushovers.

Yes, we were losing big-time. Could I keep the grin off my face? It wasn't easy.

Our new team was *special*! I watched Nosebleed drop an easy pass because he had a Kleenex pressed to his nose. Billy the Brain kept checking his laptop—trying to get *running* directions on MapQuest. Chipmunk had his hands tucked in his armpits—too shy to tackle anyone.

And Farley Mopes...Farley was the star! He kept heaving passes a mile in the air, tossing them into Pooper's Pond, into the trees, into the girls' dorm.

He was having an awesome time. I think Farley secretly dreamed of being a quarterback. And Bernie B. was happy to make his dream come true.

We were safe! We wouldn't have to play the Bone-Breakers in the championship game!

Yes, I was happy. We were forty points behind. But then I looked at my team.

My guys were hunched over, sadly shaking their heads. Feenman and Crench stared at the scoreboard, whimpering. Sharonda and the other girls covered their faces. Jennifer had tears in her eyes.

The cheerleaders sat on the grass. They didn't bother to cheer. April-May was shaking her head, muttering to herself.

Losers. We were going to be losers again. I started shaking my head, too. This wasn't right. Shouldn't we play our best game?

I looked at my friends' sad faces.

I let them down, I realized.

They all want to win. They all expected to win

this easy game. And I let them down. I made all my friends unhappy.

My heart sank to my feet. *Bernie, you can't be so selfish,* I told myself. *Bernie, these are your friends. They're counting on you.*

What's a few broken bones next week?

What's a few broken bones when your friends' happiness is at stake?

I jumped to my feet and pulled on my helmet. "Feenman! Crench! Jennifer! Let's go!" I shouted. "Let's show these clowns how to play football!"

We trotted onto the field. And The Attack of the Ecch began.

For the next half hour, Jennifer Ecch stomped and danced and pranced and stampeded, clomped and tromped over the Pushovers. And made them look like pushovers.

We finally reached the last play of the game. The score was tied 60 to 60. Only seconds left. Could we do it? Could we win the most important game of our lives?

I heaved the ball up. It bounced off Jennifer's helmet and sailed straight for—OH, NO! Farley Mopes!

"Catch it, Farley!" we all screamed. "Catch it!"

Farley slowly raised his arms. He slowly opened his hands—and TOUCHDOWN!

That *had* to go in the record books. First touchdown catch by a blind receiver!

The crowd went nuts. The cheerleaders went nuts. And even Sherman Oaks went nuts. A thrill for everybody!

Bernie B. never lets his friends down. But now the ugly truth rattled my brain. We were going to the championship game. The Bone-Breakers would be waiting for us.

Craaaaaak.
Craaaaaaaak.

My knees were hurting already!

I watched everyone celebrating on the field. I slunk away with my head down, my knees shaking.

Didn't anyone realize we were *doomed*?

Chapter 21

THE KNITTING NEEDLES FLY

I worried the whole weekend.

When Belzer brought me my breakfast on Monday morning, I could barely finish the three-egg omelet, four slices of jellied toast, hash browns, bacon and sausages, two doughnuts, a banana, and a corn muffin.

"What's wrong, Big B?" Belzer asked.

"I'm worried," I told him. "I'm very worried."

That afternoon, I saw Coach Bunz running across the grass toward me. He came bouncing up to me.

His stomach arrived first. A few seconds later, Coach Bunz caught up with it.

"Don't worry, sir," I said, giving him a sharp, two-fingered salute. "I'll whip the team into shape for the championship!"

"Sorry, Bernie. You can't do that," Coach Bunz said.

I stared at him. "What do you mean?" I said. "Why not?"

"The Bone-Breakers watched the tape of Jennifer Ecch playing against the Pushovers," he said. "Their team took a vote. They decided there was no way they could beat her."

My mouth dropped open. "You mean—?"

"After watching Jennifer play, the Bone-Breakers chose to forfeit the game. They waved the white flag, Bernie. They surrendered. Do you know what that means?"

"I get to keep my knees?" I said.

"It means WE are the state champs!" Coach Bunz cried. "We win! We're number one! We're the champs!"

He tried to jump up in the air. His stomach slapped

me a high five on the way up.

We both cheered. "Rotten Apples RULE!" I shouted.

I hurried off to tell my friends. I knew Feenman and Crench would like to carry me around on their shoulders for a while.

I saw April-May June standing with Sherman Oaks in front of the Dining Hall. I ran to tell them the good news.

"We're the state champs!" I exclaimed. "The Bone-Breakers were too *terrified* to play. So we're the *champs!*"

Sherman sneered at me. Then he turned to April-May. "I'm so *bored* with sports," he said. "All these kids getting overheated and sweaty. It's totally gross."

He took her arm. "Let's you and me go have lunch. I'll let you push the buttons on my new DVD player."

April-May spun away from him. "Sorry, Sherman," she said. "But I promised Bernie if he won the championship, I'd have lunch with *him*."

Yes! Yes! My big moment!

"Bernie, I'm so proud of you!" April-May said. She did a perfect cartwheel. "YAY, Bernie!"

I pictured myself sitting in the Dining Hall with April-May. And everyone staring at us. Maybe we'd even share a Fruit Roll-Up!

I took her arm and started to lead her up the steps. I stopped when I heard a loud cry.

"HONEY CAKES! HONEY CAKES!"

Jennifer came stomping up. She held a *huge* green, pink, and orange sweater in front of her. It was totally gross. It looked like something Cookie Monster might wear!

"Let's go, Honey Cakes," she said. "Sweater time."

Before I could move away, she raised the sweater and pulled it down over my head.

"No—please!" I begged. But I

was trapped inside it. It came
down to my knees. The arms
dragged on the ground.

And in big, red letters on the
front... inside a crooked yellow
heart... the words: BERNIE LOVES JEN.

April-May gasped. She stared at the big yellow heart. "Oh, Bernie, I didn't know!" she said. "I didn't know Jen was your girlfriend. That's so sweet. You two should have lunch together." April-May turned to leave. "Bye, Bernie."

"No! Wait—!" I shouted. I tried to cover the heart with both hands. "Wait! April-May—come back! You can't believe everything you read!"

But April-May was already walking into the Dining Hall with Sherman.

"OWWWW!" I let out a scream as Jennifer jabbed me in the butt with a knitting needle. "Move it, Honey Cakes. We've got nine sweaters to go!"

"OWWWW! Okay, okay!" I screamed. "OWW! Stop jabbing me! OWWW! Okay. I'm coming! Okay!

OWWWW!"

R.L. STINE'S

ROTTEN SCHOOL

Shake,
Rattle,
&
HURL!

THE PLOPPS

Which dorm do we Rotten House dudes hate the most?

Nyce House.

And there, at the front of the Dining Hall, stood the Nyce House Band, getting ready to play.

I saw my archenemy, that spoiled rich kid, Sherman Oaks. Sherman has no talent. He's *too rich* to bother with talent.

So he always stands to the side and shakes a tambourine. Sometimes, he hires a kid to shake the tambourine for him!

The star of the band is Sherman's good buddy, Wes Updood. Wes is maybe the best saxophone player in the universe. Even counting planets that haven't been discovered yet.

He's *that* good. He's also the coolest dude in school.

Disgusting, right?

I watched Sherman Oaks step up to a microphone. "Hello, dudes and dudettes," he boomed, tossing back his perfect blond hair. "You all know me. The one-and-only Sherman Oaks. My Nyce House band came to play for you today. No need to applaud. We know we're *way* fabulous!"

I stuck my finger down my throat and made a gagging noise.

Wes stepped up beside Sherman, carrying his saxophone. "Jack of diamonds, everyone!" he said. "Jack of diamonds, man. Silver dollars—no change!"

I told you Wes is the coolest guy in school. He's so totally cool, no one ever knows what he's *talking* about!

"Silver dollars!" Wes repeated, pumping his fist in the air. "Pudding for everyone! Blue skies, people!"

Huh? I wish I was cool enough to understand that.

Wes raised his saxophone to his mouth, and the band started to play. Kids all over the Dining Hall started to clap as music poured from Wes's sax.

His hands moved frantically over the horn. He swung it from side to side. He leaned way back and let the notes float up to the rafters. Then he ducked low, and the sounds came out like an animal growl.

As the other players kept the beat, Wes made his saxophone sing and honk and wail and cry.

I felt sick. I hated the grin on Sherman's face as he shook his tambourine, his eyes closed.

I glanced around the big room. Kids were *loving* it. My eyes stopped at the girls' table near the band. I saw April-May June rocking and bopping to the music.

April-May June—*my* girlfriend—only she doesn't know it yet. She was swaying from side to side, clapping her hands—really into it.

Oh, sick.

I had to look away. I turned to Feenman and Crench. Crench was slapping his hands to the rhythm, slapping them on Feenman's head.

"Stop it," I said. "What is the big deal here?" I had to shout over the music.

"Wes is awesome!" Feenman said, shaking his head in time to the music.

"Give me a break," I groaned. "What's so hard about playing a saxophone? You blow into it and move your fingers around. That's all there is to it."

"Wes Updood is gonna win the Talent Contest again this year," Feenman said.

I rolled my gorgeous, brown eyes. "So what?"

Feenman leaned closer. "Know what the prize is? Two tickets to see The Plopps concert. *And* you get to meet them backstage."

"The Plopps?" I started to choke. Feenman had to pound me on the back. "The P-p-plopps?" I gasped.

My heart pounded. My eyeballs started rolling around in my head.

"The Plopps?" I cried, leaping to my feet. "They're my favorite band! I've illegally downloaded every song they ever did!"

"Easy, Bernie, easy," Crench said, pulling me back down.

But I couldn't calm down. "The Plopps! The Plopps!" I cried. "Have you heard their Greatest Hits CD? *Plopping Across America?*"

I realized I was drooling.

Crench wiped my chin for me with his blazer sleeve. "Yeah," he said. "Those two Plopp sisters are *hot*."

"I can't believe Wes Updood is gonna meet them," Feenman said. "And he'll probably take his best buddy, Sherman Oaks, to the concert with him."

"No way!" I said. I jumped to my feet again. "Rotten House has *got* to win the Talent Contest this year! I'm going to that Plopps concert. No one can stop me!"

Famous last words, right?

"Bernie, we can't win the Talent Contest," Feenman said, shaking his head.

"Yeah. We've got one little problem," Crench said.

"Problem? What problem?" I asked.

They both answered together: "We don't have any TALENT!"

ABOUT THE AUTHOR

R.L. Stine graduated from Rotten School with a solid D+ average, which put him at the top of his class. He says that his favorite activities at school were Scratching Body Parts and Making Armpit Noises.

In sixth grade, R.L. won the school Athletic Award for his performance in the Wedgie Championships. Unfortunately, after the tournament, his underpants had to be surgically removed.

R.L. was very popular in school. He could tell this because kids always clapped and cheered whenever he left the room. One of his teachers remembers him fondly: "R.L. was a hard worker. He was so proud of himself when he learned to wave bye-bye with both hands."

After graduation, R.L. became well known for writing scary book series such as The Nightmare Room, Fear Street, Goosebumps, and Mostly Ghostly, and a short story collection called *Beware!*

Today, R.L. lives in a cage in New York City, where he is busy writing stories about his school days. Says he: "I wish everyone could be a Rotten Student."

For more information
about R.L. Stine,
go to www.rottenschool.com
and www.rlstine.com